Cecilia,
Be strong like Zippy!
♡ Katie Me

Dedication

To Zippy and all the fearless hummingbirds out there, especially the ones that braved the New England winter weather that year.

Zippy Allen's hummingbird in MA

LilGirl Rufous hummingbird in NH

Frosty Ruby-throated hummingbird in CT

Malia Black-chinned hummingbird in CT

Acknowledgments

To my family and friends
that encouraged me
to write this book, especially
my husband Tim.

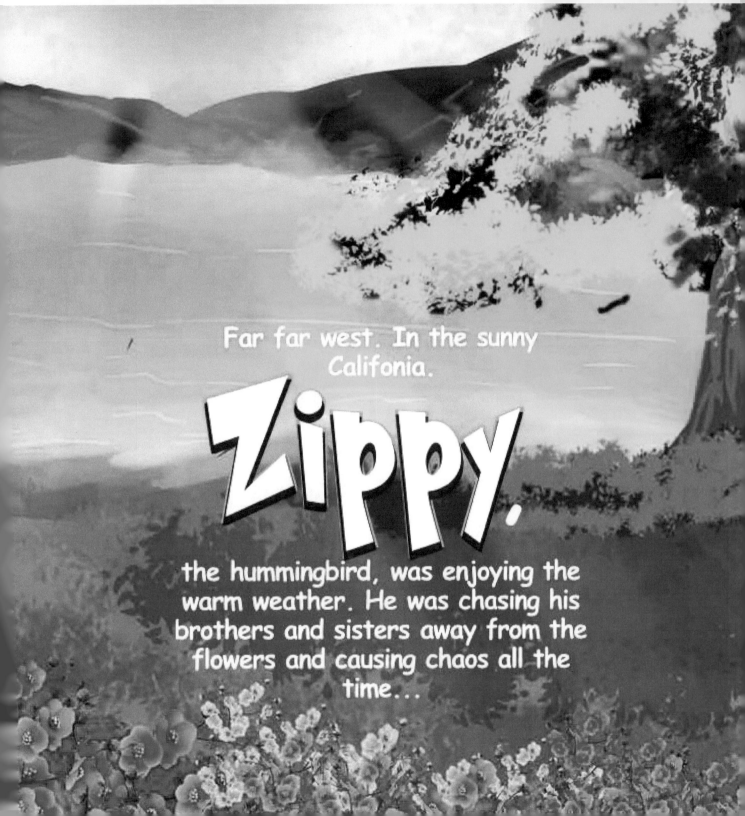

Far far west. In the sunny Califonia.

Zippy,

the hummingbird, was enjoying the warm weather. He was chasing his brothers and sisters away from the flowers and causing chaos all the time...

"**Zippy**, do you know how cold and windy
it gets over there?" Dad said.
"I am not sure about this, **Zippy**. We
are all headed south," Mom said

Zippy

had made up his mind, and he was heading East. "Hey everyone, see you in the warm south," Zippy said as he bolted off the perch to begin his long new journey. He was so excited about his adventure. Zippy was ready to spread his wings and explore the world.

Zippy
traveled for days, crossing mountains, rivers, and cities. He made it to the East Coast and even further... to the Northeast!!! Time to look for his resting spot.

All away in the Northeast, the weather was surprisingly very warm that October.

Annie

was outside enjoying the sunshine.
Plenty of flowers were in bloom, and bees
and butterflies were all around.
Hummingbirds were gone for the season.

Zippy was checking out his new garden. He saw

Annie and tried to hide behind the leaves on his perch.

"I don't think she saw me, did she? I am going for some nectar," he whispered.

Annie

was yelling, running into the house.
"What Is It, Annie?" her mother asked.
"There is a hummingbird in our garden; there is a hummingbird. I saw it, Mom, I saw It. It is brown, not green". Annie was so excited!!!

MOM, MOM,

They both hurried to the feeder. Well, there he was! A rare hummingbird in the Northeast. "What Is he doing here with cold weather on the way?"

The word spread fast, and very soon,
Zippy became a celebrity. People came
to see and photograph him all the time.
"Wow, lots of paparazzi today,"
Zippy Said.

"My name Is **Zippy**,

I am from the west coast. You never seen one like me before?" Zippy was enjoying the attention and fanning his tail left and right.

In the meantime, **Annie** was thinking about what to do on cold days as the nectar would freeze. What about the snow? It will cover the feeder. What about winds that will blow away? What about warmth for Zippy in the cold days?

Off to the store they go.
A big dome to cover the rain
and snow.
A special hummingbird feeder
to keep the nectar warm.

Light for warmth on cold winter days.
Finally, they had the
perfect setup for Zippy.

Zippy

was flying around curiously, watching Annie and her parents. They were outside, installing the new pole for the feeder to better protect it from the winter weather. They wanted to make sure that Zippy had nectar all the time.

At first, Zippy couldn't understand what humans were fussing about. The sun was shining, and the air was warm. There were still flowers in bloom.

One November night, the temperature dropped, and it was really cold. Big snowflakes covered the ground. As soon as he woke up,

Zippy went straight for the flowers. Oh no...the cold weather killed all the blooms. Zippy was so disappointed and headed for the feeder instead.

"Wow, the nectar is warm," he said. It was so nice to sip warm nectar on a cold winter day. He drank and drank for a while. Breakfast is one of the most important meals of the day for hummingbirds. In his mind, Zippy was thanking Annie and her family.

The cold weather didn't
bother
Zippy
Every day, he would fly
around and check out
new places.
Sometimes, he would
perch on his
favorite branch
close to his feeder and enjoy
the sunshine. He always kept a close eye
on the other birds and protected his yard!

Time was flying by.... On Christmas Eve, **Zippy** drank warm nectar and hung close to the warm light. He promised his family that he would meet them in the South. He had to get there fast. "Santa Is flying tonight," Zippy said. He was listening carefully for the sleigh bells.

Zippy

heard the bells! "Santa, Santa, can you give me
a ride home?".
"Hop on, Zippy," Santa said. Zippy was thankful
to Annie and her family, but he missed his.

Hummingbirds may seem fragile, but they are strong and resilient. They fly thousands of miles during spring and fall migration.

Zippy is an Allen's hummingbird that flew across the country from the West Coast, all away to Northeast Massachusetts.

Zippy keeping an eye on his feeder

Allen's hummingbirds are a rare
sight in this region. Caring
for him was a great experience.

Zippy was well taken care of with warm nectar and heat source.

Zippy was banded by a licensed professional bander. Banding helps research and understand hummingbirds and their migration patterns.

Zippy stretched his wings.

Zippy ruled the yard for several months, and on Christmas Eve, he migrated south.